KV-277-049

Townhill Primary School
DUNFERMLINE

Series consultant: Dr Terry Jennings

Designed by Jane Tassie

The author and publishers would like to thank Jordan, Georgina
and the staff and pupils of the Charles Dickens J & I School, London,
for their help in making this book. Thanks also to Colin Baldy.

A CIP record for this book is available from the British Library.

ISBN 0-7136-6328-6

First paperback edition published 2002
First published 1999 by A & C Black Publishers Limited
37 Soho Square, London W1D 3QZ
www.acblack.com

Text copyright
© 1999 Nicola Edwards and Jane Harris
Photographs copyright
© 1999 Julian Cornish-Trestrail
except for
pages 4 (main picture) and 22 (left) Greg Evans International;
page 5 (main picture) The J. Allan Cash Photolibrary;
page 23 (left) Spectrum Colour Library

All rights reserved. No part of this publication may be reproduced
or used in any form or by any means - photographic, electronic or
mechanical, including photocopying, recording, taping or
information storage and retrieval systems - without the
prior written permission of the publishers.

Typeset in 23/28pt Gill Sans Infant and 25/27 pt Soupbone Regular

Printed in Singapore by Tien Wah Press (Pte.) Ltd

A & C Black uses paper produced with elemental chlorine-free pulp,
harvested from managed sustainable forests.

Science Explorers

Sand

Exploring the science
of everyday materials

Nicola Edwards and
Jane Harris

Photographs by
Julian Cornish-Trestrail

A & C Black · London

Lots of different things are made from sand. Here are some objects that have sand in them.

There is even sand in glass.

3

In this desert, there is sand as far as you can see.

At the beach, waves break down
rocks and pebbles into sand.

A grain of
sand is a tiny
piece of rock!

I'm looking at a handful of sand through this magnifying glass.

I can see hundreds of tiny grains.

When I scoop up some sand and open my fingers, the sand runs between them. It feels smooth and cool.

Some of the sand sticks between my fingers. It feels tickly.

Watch me pour dry sand from one beaker to another.

I didn't spill any!

8

This egg-timer has sand inside it. The sand takes four minutes to pour from the top to the bottom. That's enough time to boil an egg.

Yum!

I've used a funnel to fill this bottle with sand. It feels heavy now.

When I shake it, I can't hear any noise.

I've poured out some of the sand. Now I'm going to shake the bottle again.

This time it makes a noise!

11

I'm making a sandcastle.

Oh no!
It hasn't
worked.

I'm making a sandcastle too, but my sand is wet.

My sandcastle stayed together.

We're making shapes in wet sand.

These are my footprints.

Let's try pressing these things into the sand.

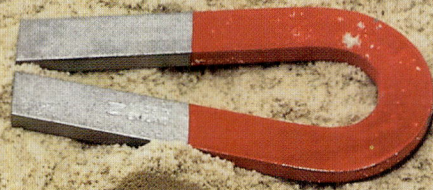

Look at all the shapes!

What will happen if we drop a marble on to each of these trays?

The marble bangs on the empty tray and rolls around.

The sand stops my marble from moving.

Now let's try standing twigs up in the trays.

In the empty tray, the twigs fall over.

The sand helps the twigs to stand up.

17

I'm planting
cress seeds.
I'm going to plant
some in soil and
some in sand.

I wonder if
the seeds will grow
in the sand?

CRESS

Cress has grown in both of the pots.

But it has grown better in the soil.

Sandpaper is paper with sand glued on to it. It feels rough.

I'm rubbing sandpaper on a plastic plate. It's scratching the plate.

Now I'm rubbing sandpaper
on this piece of wood.
The sandpaper rubs
away the rough edges.

The wood feels
smoother now.

Sand is used in building.
A builder is adding this sand
to cement in a mixer.

The cement mixture looks wet and soft. When it dries, it will hold the bricks together.

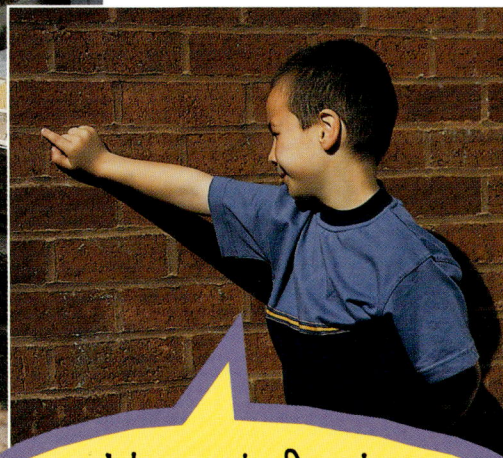

Now it feels like rock.

Notes for parents and teachers

The aim of the *Science Explorers* series is to introduce children to ways of observing and classifying materials, so that they can discover the various properties which make them suitable for a range of uses. By talking about what they already know about materials from their everyday use of different objects, the children will gain confidence in making predictions about how a material will behave in different circumstances. Through their explorations, the children will be able to try out their ideas in a fair test.

pp 2–5

Sand is made up of tiny particles of a mixture of minerals, including quartz, feldspar, magnetite and mica. Created by the erosion of rocks, sand is carried by wind and water and deposited on beaches, in deserts and along the banks of lakes and rivers. Sand occurs naturally in a variety of colours, depending on the rock from which it originates (for example, black sand formed from basalt is found in volcanic areas).

Discuss the children's experience of sand: at school, at home, on building sites and on holiday. How would they describe sand? What do they like doing with it? Show the children objects that contain sand (such as sand bricks, sandpaper, egg-timers and glass), and compare the raw material with the finished products.

pp 6–8

Encourage the children to study a pinch of sand with a magnifying glass and, if possible, under a microscope. Can they separate out a single grain of sand?

The children could try transferring sand from one container to another, using paper and plastic bags, wooden boxes, metal pots, plastic jugs and so on. They could investigate which shapes and materials are most suitable and why. This activity also provides an opportunity to investigate capacity. Which container do the children think will hold the most sand? Discuss their predictions and ask them how they could record their findings. If possible, provide the children with coarse- and fine-grained sand and ask them to compare the look and feel of each. They could consider how each type of sand behaves in the investigations featured in the book.

p 9

Provide the children with a variety of timing devices, for example, sand glasses, egg-timers, stopwatches, clocks and kitchen timers. Ask them to compare the effectiveness of each. Can they identify the limitations of a sand glass as a means of timing?

pp 10–11

Can the children think why the sand in the half-full bottle makes a noise when they shake it, whereas the tightly packed sand makes no noise?

pp 12–15

Provide the children with sand, water and a variety of buckets, spades, plastic moulds and watering cans.

Encourage them to investigate how wet the sand needs to be to make the best moulded shapes. How do they know when they've added too much water?

The children could also investigate how much weight a sandcastle can bear before it collapses, for example by placing a succession of plastic building blocks on top of the sandcastle until it gives way.

pp 16–17

The children could compare the bolstering effect of sand with a variety of other substances, for example, water, flour, sugar and cotton wool. Discuss with the children how sandbags are used to offer protection against rising floodwater.

pp 18–19

While sandy soil provides a growing medium which combines good drainage with the necessary nutrients for plant growth, sand alone does not contain the right nutrients for healthy growth. Discuss the conditions which need to be in place for a plant to grow and thrive. The children may have seen grass growing on sand dunes or trailing plants at the edges of beaches in tropical countries.

pp 20–21

The children could test the abrasive effect of sandpaper on a variety of materials, such as metal, stone, plastic, wood, wool and cotton fabric.

pp 22–23

The children may have seen sand and cement being mixed in concrete mixers, in their local area or on television. You could read with them *The Big Concrete Lorry* by Shirley Hughes (Walker Books). If possible, demonstrate with a small quantity of sand, water and cement how the mixture changes and sets as the ingredients react with each other.

Find the page

Here are some of the words and ideas in this book.